Sam's Wish

SAVIOUR PIROTTA

Illustrated by
Valeria Szucs

This is Samira. Samira lives with her mum, her dad and her younger brother, Anish.

Samira is good at many things. She is good at maths, science and painting. She is good at reading, and she loves reading stories about magic worlds.

Samira is also very good at helping other people. Sometimes she wishes she could escape to one of those magic worlds that she reads about just so that she can have a little bit of a rest from putting others first all the time.

Like the time her grandparents come to visit.

The day before they arrive her mum says, "Grandma and Grandpa will get here very early on Saturday."

"They'll be hungry," says Samira right away. "I'll make them beans on toast. It's Grandpa's favourite breakfast."

Before going to bed, Samira checks she has everything ready for the breakfast. Sliced bread. Butter. Baked beans. Brown sauce. Brown sauce is Grandma's favourite. Samira remembers from the last visit.

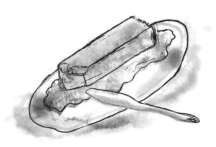

"You must go to bed or you'll be too tired in the morning," says Mum. "I'll wake you up when Grandma and Grandpa get here."

Samira gives Mum a goodnight hug. "Sleep tight," says Mum.

But Samira is too excited to fall asleep. The clock on the bedside table ticks very loudly. Samira is still counting the ticks of the clock when she hears a car outside.

Car doors slam. A suitcase on
wheels is dragged up the driveway.

Samira flies down the stairs. "Hello, Grandma. Hello, Grandpa."

Grandpa sweeps Samira up in his powerful arms. "Hello, flower. You've grown."

"Are you hungry?" says Samira.
"Do you want some breakfast?"
   "We're starving after that long
drive," laughs Grandma.

Samira puts bread in the toaster. She switches the kettle on. She opens the cupboard to get the beans.

"They're gone!" she cries. "Someone ate my beans."

"I'm afraid that was me," says Dad.
"I had a snack when I came in late
from work. Are there no more?"

"Samira can get some more from the corner shop," says Mum.

Samira gasps. She never goes to the corner shop. In fact, she always crosses the street when she walks past it. Mrs April, the woman who runs the shop, has a lazy eye. Samira is never sure if she is looking at her or someone else. Samira thinks Mrs April might be a witch.

"I'll come with you, Samira,"
says Grandpa, who can see
she looks worried.

Mrs April's shop is a jumble of tins and boxes. There are cats sitting on everything. The fridge at the back makes hissing noises, like a dragon in disguise.

HISSsssss

"I've got one tin of beans left," says Mrs April, reaching for a top shelf. "And it's very special. Use it wisely." She smiles.

It's true she has a lazy eye, but her smile is very friendly. Samira is not worried anymore.

"What did Mrs April mean, the beans are very special?" Samira asks Grandpa on the way home.

Grandpa looks at the tin closely. "There's a special offer on these beans. A wish comes true with every mouthful!"

"That must be a joke," says Mum,
when Samira and Grandpa get home.
"Magic wishes indeed."

"But it *is* true," Samira wants to say.
"Mrs April's shop is magic."

"We'll see," says Grandpa. He pulls
on the ring pull and spoons out a
helping of beans. "Go on, Samira.
Make a wish."

"You go first," says Samira, kindly. "After all, it's your breakfast."

Grandpa puts the spoon into his mouth and mutters a wish. There is a whoosh and a thump! A brand new book appears out of nowhere and lands on the kitchen table.

Everyone stares at it with their mouths wide open.

"Well, I never," says Grandpa.

"That was a waste of a good wish, if you ask me," snorts Grandma. "You can get a book free from the library."

"Let me make a wish," says Anish. Before anyone can stop him, he thrusts the spoon into his mouth. There's a whoosh, a thump, and the jangle of a bicycle bell. A brand new bike whizzes into the kitchen.

"Cool," says Anish.

"I think Samira should make the next wish," says Grandpa. "After all, she bought the beans."

But Grandma grabs the beans before Samira can get them. Samira can see her lips moving as she makes a wish.

Suddenly there is a whoosh, a thump, the jangle of a bicycle bell – and a neigh. A racing horse trots out of the hallway.

"Goodness!" cries Mum. "Where are we going to keep a horse?"

"It's this house that's the problem, not the horse," says Grandma. "I've always said it's too small." She passes Mum the beans. "You've always aimed too low. Now do something right for once."

Mum chews on a mouthful of beans carefully. There's a whoosh, a thump, the jangle of a bicycle bell, a neigh, and – the creak of floorboards stretching. Suddenly, the house is ten times bigger. It's like a palace, Samira thinks.

"This is more like it!" cries Grandma. "I hope you wished for stables to go with the house."

She's about to open the door when Dad comes in, grumbling. "Can't anyone get some sleep in here?"

He stares at the huge room and the horse. "Am I dreaming?"

Grandma thrusts the tin of beans under his nose. "Make a wish, son."

Everyone seems to have forgotten that the beans are Samira's and that she hasn't made a wish yet. And she's just too shy to remind them.

Dad's about to eat some beans when they hear shouting outside. Samira runs to the window. The people from next door are marching up the driveway.

"Where are your parents?" they roar,
seeing Samira at the window. "Your silly
house has squashed ours flat."

Samira stares through the window.
The houses all round are squashed up,
like sardines in a can. "This is not good,"
she says. "I'll get Mum."

But the neighbours open the front door and pile into the kitchen.

"Calm down, everyone!" yells Grandma, waving the tin of beans around. "You can all get a big house like ours. All you have to do is wish."

"Please," says Samira, desperately. "We're wasting the wishes."

But no one takes any notice. The tin is snatched this way and that.

"I wish for a house twice as big as this one," says one of the neighbours.

"And I wish for a house ten times as big," laughs another.

The wishes get more and more ridiculous. Someone wishes for an actual palace.

Someone else wishes for a jumbo jet.
Soon there is a big fight about whose turn
it is next. The tin of beans is hurled
right out of the window.

"Oh no!" cries Samira. She runs outside to rescue the tin. It's landed in a muddy patch and there are no beans left. "Now I'll never make my wish come true," says Samira.

"Perhaps Mrs April will find another tin," says Grandpa.

But Mrs April shakes her head. "I'm afraid that really was the last one."

"I shouldn't have let everyone make a wish," says Samira. "The whole estate is ruined and it's all my fault."

"Let me have a look at that tin, dear," says Mrs April, gently.

She bends the lid up to see underneath it. "Oh look, there's one little bean left. It's squashed, but I'm sure it will make one last wish come true. Only a little wish, I should think."

Samira knows exactly what kind of wish she wants to make. She scoops up the bean with the tip of her finger and pops it into her mouth. "I wish..."

There's a jumble of loud noise, followed by a neigh, the jangle of a bicycle bell, a thump, a whoosh, and suddenly the tin of beans flies onto the counter. It isn't open yet.

"That's an amazing wish!" cries Grandpa. "Now we can start all over again."

"Clever girl," says Mrs April, and her cats all wave their tails very fast.

Outside, everything is calm and quiet. All the houses are back to their original size. There's no jumbo jet parked in the playing area. "It's like the magic wishes never happened," says Grandpa.

"Phew!" says Samira. "I'm glad I sorted everything out in the end. But let's not tell anyone about the magic beans this time. We'll pretend we changed our minds about beans on toast for breakfast."

"Yes," Grandpa agrees. "We'll keep the tin a secret until we're sure everyone can wish sensibly."

"And this time *I'm* going to make the first wish," says Samira.

"Good girl," says Grandpa. "It's about time you put yourself first for once. What will you wish for?"

"Now that," says Samira with a little skip and a smile, "is a secret! You'll just have to wait and see."

Fun Facts About Baked Beans

Heinz introduced baked beans to the UK in 1901 where they were sold by posh London department store, Fortnum & Mason, as a luxury item.

There are approximately 465 beans in a standard 415g can of Heinz Beanz.

Although Samira uses cannellini beans in her special beans on toast recipe, Heinz uses a type of haricot bean called the 'navy' bean.

The other main ingredient is tomato purée, made with Mediterranean-grown tomatoes. Heinz uses enough tomatoes every day to fill an Olympic-size swimming pool.

In 2014 in the House of Lords, the energy minister was asked whether smelly emissions from eating baked beans contributed to global warming!

One cup of baked beans contains the same amount of protein as 12 eggs.

More than one and a half million cans of baked beans are sold every day in the UK alone. During the Covid-19 pandemic lockdown, sales of baked beans increased by 50%.

SAMIRA'S MAGIC BEANS ON TOAST

Ingredients *

1 can of cannellini beans (400g), drained and rinsed

Tomato passata (200g)

1 small brown onion, finely chopped

150ml vegetable stock

Henderson's Relish (15ml)

1 tsp sugar (optional)

40g Cheddar cheese, grated

1 spring onion, finely sliced (optional)

Olive oil and salt

1. Soften the brown onion in a medium pan with a drizzle of olive oil and a pinch of salt.

2. Add the cannellini beans, tomato passata, vegetable stock, Henderson's Relish and the sugar to the pan.

3. Stir everything together and bring to the boil over a high heat.

4. Simmer for about 5 minutes until the mixture has thickened.

5. Serve on top of a slice of toast sprinkled with the Cheddar (and spring onions).

* beware any allergens!

WACKÝ BEE

Published by
Wacky Bee Books
Shakespeare House, 168 Lavender Hill, London, SW11 5TG, UK

ISBN: 978-1-913292-07-2

First published in the UK 2020

Design by David Rose

Picture credits: iStockphoto.com

Printed by ADverts, Latvia

www.wackybeebooks.com